Buttercup the Moon

About the story

All the animal friends notice
the moon is looking smaller in
the night sky. Has Buttercup
the old brown cow jumped up
and eaten the moon?

Buttercup and the Moon

Once upon a time Reynard the Fox and Sharp-eye the Weasel looked up into the sky and noticed that the moon was only half a moon.

"It was a big round moon not so many nights ago," said Reynard. "It was fine to hunt by because it gave so much light. What has happened to it?"

"It keeps going like that," said Sharp-eye the Weasel.

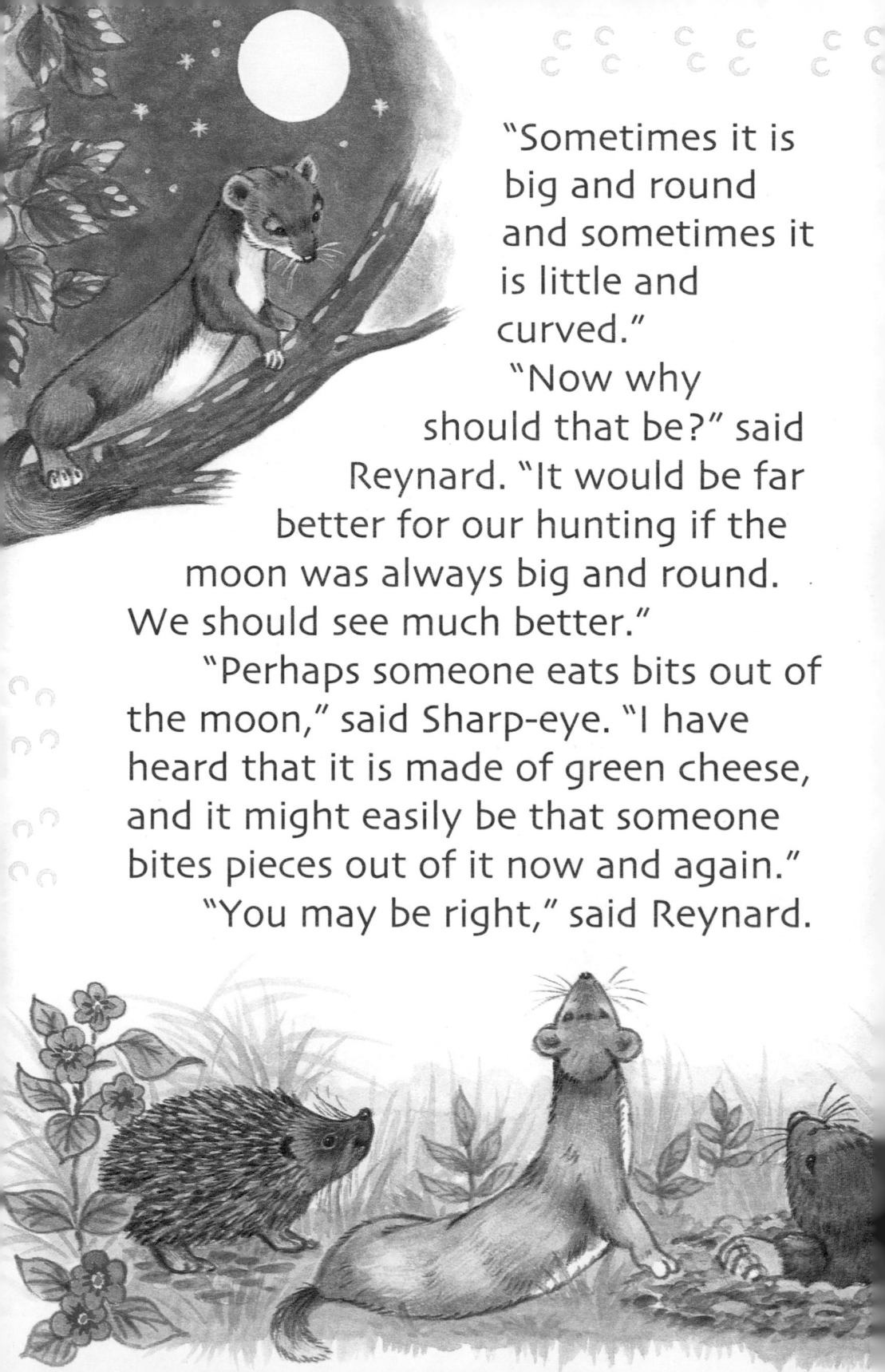

"Sometimes it is big and round and sometimes it is little and curved."

"Now why should that be?" said Reynard. "It would be far better for our hunting if the moon was always big and round. We should see much better."

"Perhaps someone eats bits out of the moon," said Sharp-eye. "I have heard that it is made of green cheese, and it might easily be that someone bites pieces out of it now and again."

"You may be right," said Reynard.

"Let us call a meeting and find out who eats the moon."

So they called a meeting and all the animals came – the rabbit, the hare, the mole, the stoat, the hedgehog, and the bat.

"Someone eats the moon," said Reynard solemnly. "We must find out who it is and stop them. Who could it be?"

Everybody thought hard. Then Long-ears the grey Rabbit, spoke.

"You know there is a rhyme about the cow jumping over the moon," he said. "Now why should a cow do such a thing! Why, to take a bite out of it as she jumps, of course!"

Everyone clapped at this. They thought it was a very good guess.

"You must be right," said Reynard. "I will see the cow about it."

"We will come with you," said all

7

the animals. So off they went to the field where Buttercup, the old brown cow, was lying down asleep. She was surprised to find such a crowd round her when she awoke.

"What do you want?" she asked.

"We want to know why you keep eating the moon," said Reynard sternly.

"Whatever do you mean?" asked Buttercup in astonishment. "Eat the moon! Whatever next? Why, I have plenty of sweet grass without bothering about a silly thing like the moon!"

"We don't believe you," said Reynard. "Listen, Buttercup! If you eat the moon any more we will chain you up in a dark shed and you will not be allowed on the sunny hillside again."

The cow tossed her head and flicked her tail at the fox.

"Silly creature," she said. "Go away. I tell you I *don't* eat the moon."

"Well, remember we have warned you!" said Reynard, and he and all the animals went away.

Now the next night was cloudy and the moon only showed itself once, then it disappeared. The animals felt certain that Buttercup had jumped up into the sky and eaten up every bit of the moon. They were angry, for they thought that if the moon was eaten all up it would never grow again.

"Fetch a chain and we will tie up the cow in a shed," said Reynard. "Then she can do no more damage. She will eat the stars next, the greedy creature."

So a strong chain was fetched and they all set off for Buttercup's field.

They put the chain round her neck, and made her walk down the hill until she came to a dark shed. They took her inside and chained her up.

"Now you can do no more harm!" they said. "Leave the sky alone, you wicked cow. You have eaten the moon all up and we shall never see it again."

The poor cow wept and sighed, but it was of no use. She could not get free, so she had to lie down

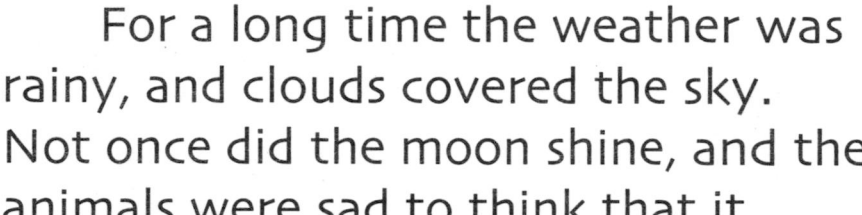

and make the
best of things.
But how she
missed the
windy hillside
and the sweet
green grass!

For a long time the weather was rainy, and clouds covered the sky. Not once did the moon shine, and the animals were sad to think that it should all be eaten.

"We will have the cow out tonight, and decide what to do to punish her for such a dreadful deed," said Reynard. So that night Buttercup was taken out of the shed, and set in the middle of a ring with all the animals sitting round her. She was very sad and hung her big brown head.

"Now," said Reynard, standing up, "we have come here to decide what punishment to give the prisoner for daring to eat our lovely moon. Never more will it shine down to give us light – the greedy cow you see before you has gobbled it all up!"

And then, at that very moment the silver moon sailed out from behind a cloud and shone down on all the animals below! She was quite full, very round and very bright, and she seemed to smile at everyone.

"Look!" said the cow. "There is the moon! Why do you say I have eaten her? You are very unkind to me. I wouldn't do any harm to such a beautiful thing. If I had eaten her she wouldn't be in the sky, would she?"

All the animals went red and looked at one another. The cow was quite right. She could not have eaten the moon if it was still in the sky. What a strange thing!

"You are free," said Reynard, and he took the chain from Buttercup's neck. She ran off to her field, mooing gladly, and began to nibble the green grass in delight.

"The moon is a mystery," said Long-ears the Rabbit. "Let us be thankful we have it, whether large or small, round or like a slice of melon. She comes when she will, we none of us know why!"

"There is a book in the schoolroom down in the village which tells all about the moon," said Prickles the Hedgehog.

"Who can read?" asked Reynard. But nobody could, and one by one all the animals slipped away. Reynard was left alone, looking up at the silver moon. She seemed to laugh at him, and he grew angry.

"I'll eat you myself! I'll eat you myself," he cried.

He leapt high into the air, but he could not reach the moon. He jumped again, but it was no use – the moon sailed in the sky, and took no notice of him at all.

"Moo, moo!" suddenly said Buttercup, looking over the hedge. "So you're the one that jumps at the moon and nibbles it, are you? Moo, moo!"

Then Reynard ran away as fast as his four legs would take him, and he never dared to go near Buttercup again, in case she told tales of him. But it would have served him right if she had, wouldn't it?

About the Storyteller
Enid Blyton

Enid Blyton wrote poems, stories and plays to amuse herself as a young girl, and after training as a kindergarten teacher she had her first book published.

In all, Enid Blyton wrote around 700 books, including The Famous Five, Malory Towers, The Magic Faraway Tree and Noddy.

Today, her books are available in more than 40 languages and films, television series, video and audio cassettes, CD ROMs and other merchandise, ensuring that she remains the world's favourite children's author.

About the Illustrator
Sylvia A Ward

On leaving school at 15, Sylvia joined County Studio as a trainee illustrator. Over the years she has developed her style of work to include licensed properties for American and UK publishers as well as greeting card and gift wrap designs.

She has designed and produced patterns for Tiffany style stained glass panels. Her hobbies include hand engraving glassware in her own style and design, also collecting curios.